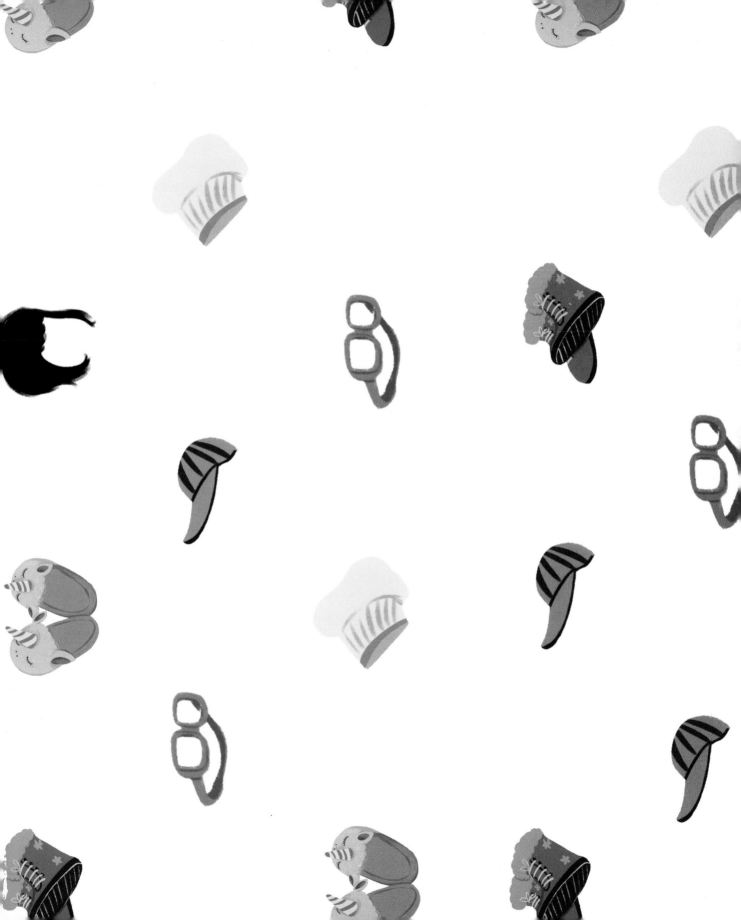

For my mommy, thank you.

ISBN: 978-0-578-32298-8 (Hardcover)

Printed by Walsworth, in the United States of America.
First printing 2021.
HMJ Publishing
PO Box 16080
Chicago, IL 60616

www.heymissjohnson.com

Many Hats

WRITTEN BY
SHANNON JOHNSON

ILLUSTRATED BY
SAWYER CLOUD

HMJ
Publishing
HEY MISS JOHNSON

It was Friday afternoon, which meant that
Zoey's dad was picking her up from school.
Zoey loved the time they spent together
before her mommy got home with the twins.

This Friday was extra special because all the students got to wear their favorite pajamas to school.

Zoey couldn't wait for her dad to see her outfit, even though it hadn't quite turned out the way she had planned.

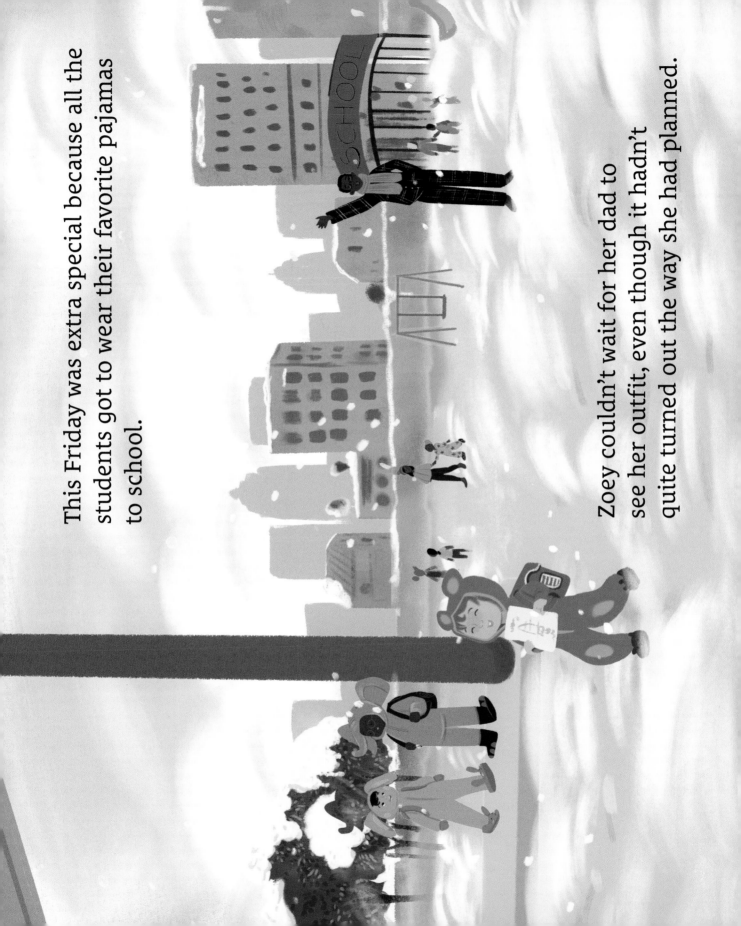

"How was school today, Princess?" asked Dad.

"Well, Mommy forgot to pack my new slippers for Pajama Day, and I was the only kid in the class wearing pink unicorn jammies . . . with snow boots!" Zoey pouted.

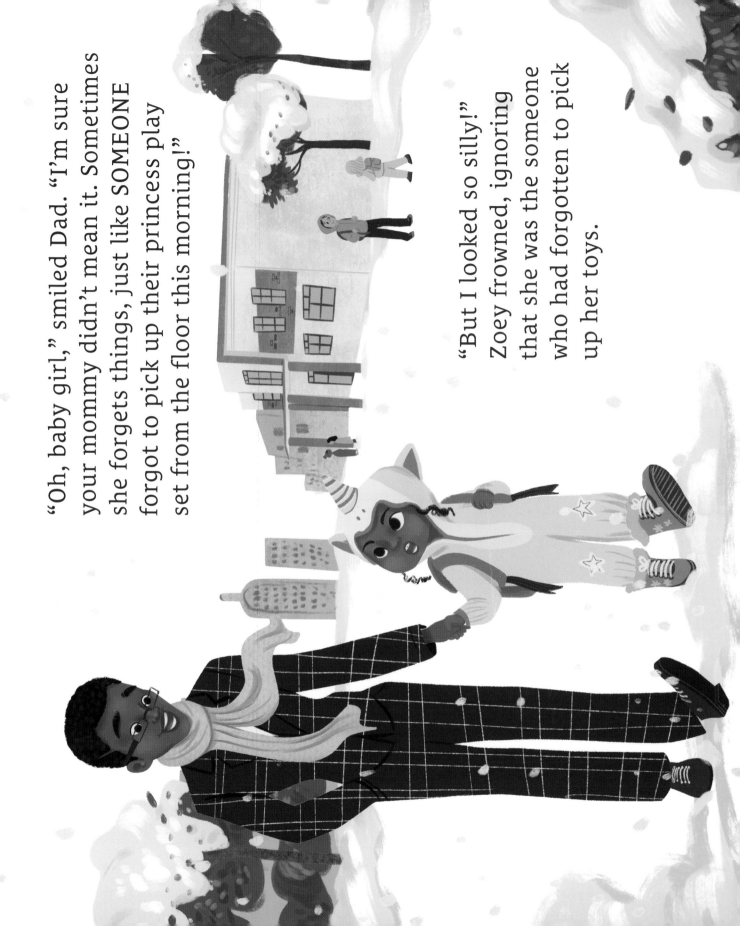

"Oh, baby girl," smiled Dad. "I'm sure your mommy didn't mean it. Sometimes she forgets things, just like SOMEONE forgot to pick up their princess play set from the floor this morning!"

"But I looked so silly!" Zoey frowned, ignoring that she was the someone who had forgotten to pick up her toys.

Zoey folded her arms and rolled her eyes the way she always does when she's upset.

"I think your PJ's look great!" said Dad. "Try to give your mommy a break. She wears many hats."

"What do Mommy's hats have to do with my unicorn slippers?" Zoey asked.

"Wearing many hats means that she has a lot on her plate," Dad replied.

"What does that mean?" said Zoey, more confused than ever. "Mommy doesn't even eat a lot!"

"Well, not only is she your mommy, but she's also a vet, and the assistant soccer coach," said Dad. "She does a lot for us, so she has a lot to remember."

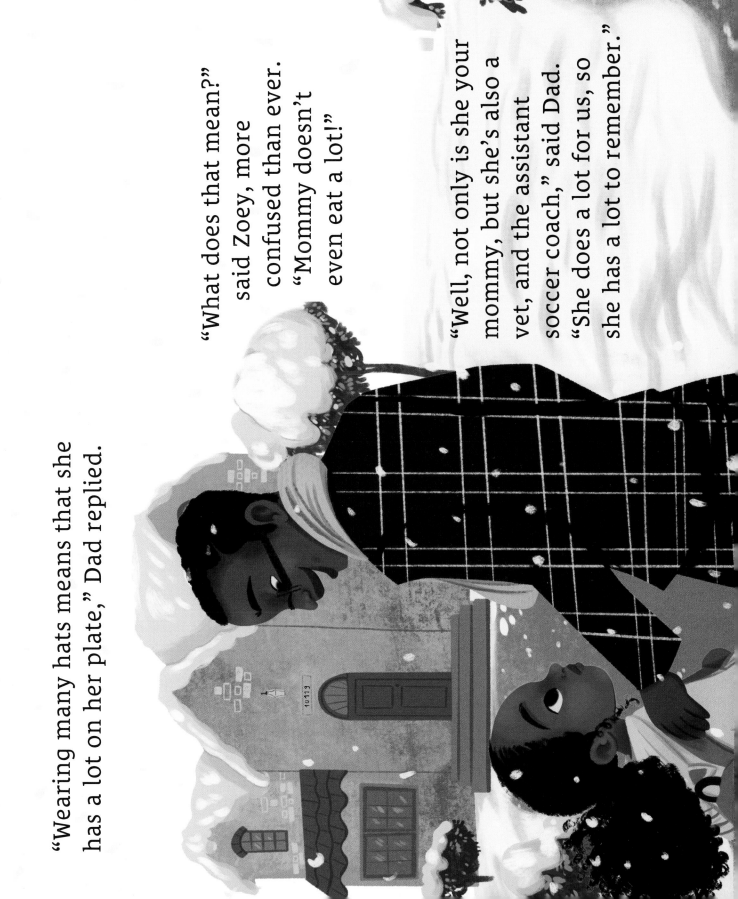

"Why don't you hang up your things while I make us a little snack?" Dad said as they arrived at home.

As Zoey put her coat away, she thought about when Max had chewed her shoes. Her mommy built cubbies for her and the twins and decorated them.

"Now you each have your own space where Max can't get your things!" she smiled. Zoey's mommy must have been wearing her construction hat that day! She always knows just what to do.

Zoey and her dad sat down for a snack and shared stories about her mommy's many hats.

Like the time Zoey tried to conquer the tallest, swirliest slide at the park while her mommy was busy teaching the twins how to ride their bikes.

Things didn't quite go as planned with the slide, but Zoey's mommy was right there with her nurse hat, a first-aid kit and lots of kisses.

Dad reminded Zoey about the time her mommy spent hours styling her hair for Picture Day, even though she still had to make dinner and pack their lunches.

"Mommy made sure that my ponytails were perfect!" smiled Zoey. "She's so much better at making them than you, Dad."

Zoey's mind raced with thoughts of the many hats her mommy wears.

She imagined her in a chef's hat on a Wednesday night. She makes the BEST spaghetti!

And as a referee, because the twins are always fighting over their toys!

Then she thought about the time her mommy helped her brothers win the science fair. They made the best volcano anyone had ever seen!

But, best of all, Zoey liked her mommy's Game Night hat. She was the family karaoke champ, and she always made everyone laugh with her costumes.

Thinking about all of those hats made Zoey realize just how much her mommy did for their family.

Zoey wanted to do something to show her how much she loved and appreciated her.

So she ran over to her backpack
to get some art supplies.
As Zoey rummaged
through her things,
she found something
very unexpected . . . .

"My unicorn slippers!" she shouted.

Zoey remembered her mommy telling her to put them in her bag last night before school. "Mommy isn't the only one who forgets things!" she said.

With some help from Dad, Zoey got started cutting, painting, and glittering.

She knew her mommy would love her surprise!

Just then, Zoey's mommy came home from work with the twins. When she saw Zoey's unicorn pajamas, she sighed. "I'm so sorry, Princess. I was in such a rush this morning that I forgot to pack your slippers."

Zoey quickly replied, "You didn't! It was me who forgot that they were in my backpack! I know you have a lot of things to juggle, Mommy, so we are going to help out more from now on!"

Zoey and her brothers put away the groceries while Dad finished up dinner. "No chores for you tonight!" he said to Zoey's mommy. "You just relax."

"And Mason and Jackson can take out the trash!" she added. Her brothers were surprisingly happy to help.

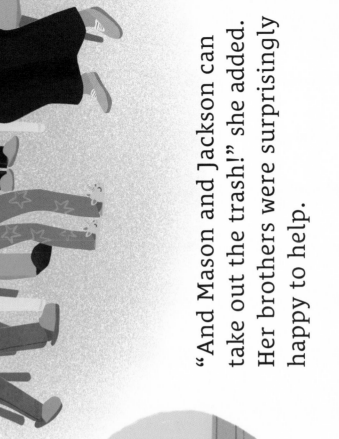

After dinner, Zoey's mommy started to gather the dirty plates. Zoey jumped up. "I'll do that!" she said.

Once the kitchen was spotless,
Dad had a surprise for everyone.
"How about my famous chocolate
brownies for dessert?" he smiled.

Zoey had another
surprise as she handed
her mommy an envelope
covered in purple glitter.

"I know you already have a lot of hats to wear," said Zoey, "but I think you'll like this one."

Her mommy pulled out the thank you hat and smiled. "I love it!" she said. Zoey gave her the biggest hug that her little five-year-old arms could.

"There's just one thing," said Zoey's mommy . . .

"We'll have to share this hat.
Because I am thankful for all of you, too."